Sue Mongredien

Illustrated by Maria Pearson

For Rebecca Hill and Sarah Stewart –
thank you!

First published in the UK in 2009 by Usborne Publishing Ltd., Usborne House,
83-85 Saffron Hill, London EC1N 8RT, England. www.usborne.com

A CIP catalogue record for this book is available from the British Library.

This edition published in America in 2016 AE.
PB ISBN 9780794536848 ALB ISBN 9781601304100
JFMAMJJASO D/20 01528-9
Printed in China

Contents

The Mermaids of th
Molly
Ella
Delphi
Shivana

Undersea Kingdom
Coral
Queen Luna
Princess Silva
Pearl

"Ten more minutes before it's time to get ready for bed, Molly," Mrs. Holmes said, taking dry laundry off the line in the backyard. "Molly? Are you listening?"

Molly was lying in the hammock her dad had put up between the two old apple trees. She looked up and blinked at her mom's words. She'd been reading a book her gran had loaned her about creatures living at the

North and South Poles and was almost surprised to see that she was in the warm backyard with sweetly-scented flowers blooming around her in the evening sun, rather than knee-deep in crisp snow. "Um... okay, Mom," she said. "Hey, listen to this: did you know that all polar bears are left-handed?"

Mrs. Holmes folded a clean white sheet over her arm and raised an eyebrow. "Shouldn't that be left-pawed?" she joked.

Molly smiled and turned the page of her book. *Polar Bears in Danger*, she read at the top of the next page. She felt her smile vanish as she read on. It said that the polar bear was an endangered species, because the ice floes of the Arctic were melting. Without the huge glaciers to live and hunt on, the polar bear would quickly become extinct.

Molly stared at the picture of a snowy-white cub frolicking with its mother, and felt sad. Polar bears were such beautiful animals – she hated the thought of them being in danger.

She turned to the next page, where there was a photo of a shaggy white polar bear swimming through the sea, with glaciers like icy mountains all around it. The bear's head was out of the water, while its great legs paddled below the surface. It looked almost as if it was smiling, its black nose sniffing the air, its dark eyes half-closed.

Molly glanced over her right shoulder, where she could just see the sea sparkling down below in Horseshoe Bay. It had been another sunny day there, and the sea had been warm enough to swim in. She couldn't imagine what it would be like to be a polar bear, swimming in water so freezing cold that chunks of ice floated around you!

Although… She smiled as she thought of something. She had met someone who *did* swim in such icy seas, of course: Shivana, the Shell-Keeper mermaid who looked after the ocean's frozen wastes. Molly had met Shivana when some extraordinary magic had taken her deep into the Undersea Kingdom for the very first time…

"Five minutes, Molly," her mom said at that moment, balancing the basket of laundry on her hip as she turned to go back into the cottage.

"All right," Molly replied. Her fingers closed absent-mindedly around the creamy-pink piece of shell that dangled from a chain around her neck. Gran had given Molly the necklace when Molly and her family had moved in to live with her in Horseshoe Bay, and Molly had quickly discovered that the shell had magical powers. It sometimes turned her into a mermaid at night!

Not only that, but her shell had once been part of a larger conch shell – and five other mermaids also had pieces of it, which helped them protect different parts of the ocean.

Molly couldn't help wondering if the glaciers were melting more quickly because Shivana didn't have her piece of the special magical shell any more. A bad mermaid known as Carlotta the Dark Queen had stolen the conch pieces from the Shell-Keeper mermaids to use their magic for herself, and Molly had been helping her new friends get them back.

"Are you all right there, Molls? You haven't nodded off already, have you?"

Molly jerked her head around at her dad's voice. He'd come out into the backyard with his newspaper. "I'm fine," she told him. "Just thinking."

He checked his watch. "I reckon you should think about putting your pajamas on," he said. "Mom and I will come up in a few minutes and tuck you in, okay?"

Molly nodded, swung her legs out of her hammock and walked across the lawn, the cool grass tickling her bare toes. Inside the cottage, she kissed her gran goodnight before going upstairs, tiptoeing past the tiny room where her baby brother slept, and into her own room.

She pulled on her pajamas quickly, setting her shell necklace on her bedside table as usual. She never could tell when its magic would work, but she was really hoping she'd find herself in the Undersea Kingdom tonight. She was dying to know what was happening down there! The stolen pieces of the conch shell had magically left the Dark Queen and had been scattered all around the ocean, and Molly's friends had been racing to find their pieces before the Dark Queen could get her hands on them again. In fact, Shivana's was the only piece left missing. What if Carlotta had tracked it down already?

She suppressed a shiver at the thought. Her parents came in to kiss her goodnight just then,

and Molly snuggled down under her quilt when they'd gone, her mind still racing with questions. She had never met the Dark Queen herself, but had encountered lots of creatures which had been enslaved into her army of followers – and a very scary bunch they were too, all with sinister red eyes. If the Dark Queen had managed to find Shivana's piece of the shell again, she could be working some terrible magic in the coldest areas of the ocean...

Molly closed her eyes and wiggled into a more comfortable position, hugging the pillow under her head. And then suddenly it seemed as if the bed was dissolving beneath her and Molly was falling down...down...down...

There was a tingling sensation in her legs as if they were melting, and moments later she felt cool water against her skin. She was the secret mermaid again!

The tingling feeling vanished as suddenly as it had begun, and Molly opened her eyes. Yes – she was underwater, and there was her beautiful green mermaid tail in the place where her legs had been! She gave it a flick and surged through the sea, smiling with happiness as her hair streamed out behind her. Oh, it was wonderful to be back in the Undersea Kingdom!

She looked about expectantly. Every time she'd become a mermaid so far, she'd appeared near one of the Shell-Keeper mermaids. This time, however, there was no one in sight. The water was a clear blue, and very cold, and the light seemed strange and eerie, filtering down in dim shafts at intervals. Then she looked up and gasped. There was a ceiling of thick ribbed ice above her head! Was she in the Arctic Ocean? Or maybe the Antarctic?

"Shivana?" she called hesitantly. There was no sign of the red-haired mermaid, though, just a school of silvery fish that appeared from out of nowhere, and a fat cinnamon-colored walrus swimming some distance away, its stout flippers sending it along at a surprising speed. Molly watched curiously as it swam to an open section of sea where the sunlight fell in, then heaved itself out of the water. She gazed down at the seabed and saw rocks and bare sand beneath her. Was it too cold even for seaweed to grow here?

"I guess I'd better explore," she said to herself after a few moments. Her magical shell must have brought her to this place for a reason, she decided, setting off through the water. Maybe she'd find Shivana's piece of the conch shell all on her own. Or maybe...

Molly froze as a sound reached her ears. A faint, muffled sound – rather like a cry. "Shivana?" she called out, louder this time. She swam in the direction of the voice. "Shivana, is that you?"

The voice was more distinct this time, and Molly's blood ran cold as she realized what was being shouted.

"Help! Somebody help me!"

Molly pushed hard with her tail fin to send herself shooting through the chilly sea at top speed. She moved out from under the ice ceiling to a lighter, warmer patch of water, where lumps of ice shifted and bobbed about above her head. Who was shouting for help? Was it Shivana? She couldn't see any sight of her mermaid friend, despite looking frantically in all directions. Was somebody else in trouble, maybe?

"Where are you?" she called helplessly, searching everywhere as she swam.

Another school of silvery fish darted past like a stream of mercury, and Molly had to swerve aside to avoid them. She was in a deeper area of water now, with lots of dark shadowy rocks below her.

"Here! In this cave!" the voice came again. "Molly – is that you?"

"Yes!" Molly replied, swimming toward the voice. A cave? She couldn't see any cave. "But I can't—" She broke off as she spotted a dark opening in the rocks nearby. There was a hollow – was that the cave? She drew closer and saw that the opening did become wider and deeper and that, yes, there *was* a rocky chamber within. But a gate made of long icicles, like bars, prevented her from going any further inside it.

To Molly's horror, Shivana was trapped behind the icicles like a prisoner! Molly had been in awe of the flame-haired mermaid when she'd met her before – she was so forthright and businesslike. But now she looked pale and frightened, her dark eyes wide with shock as she clung to the icy bars of her prison. "Molly, thank goodness you're here!" she cried, stretching a hand through to clutch at her. "Terrible things have been happening!"

"Who did this to you?" Molly asked. "Was it the Dark Queen?"

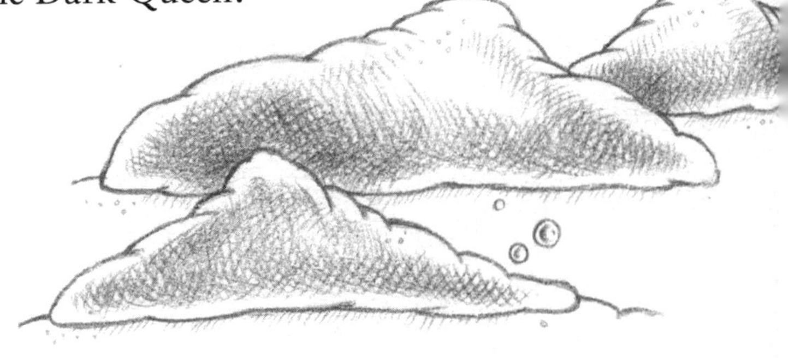

Shivana shook her head, her red ringlets bouncing around her face. "No," she said. "It was Princess Silva!"

Molly stared in surprise. "Princess *Silva*?" she echoed. The princess was the daughter of Queen Luna, the Merqueen, who was the kindest and most gracious person Molly had ever met.

"Yes," Shivana replied with a shiver. "I'd just found my piece of the conch shell, in the depths of an icy canyon, and was about to take it to show the Merqueen, when all of a sudden a huge octopus with glowing red eyes pounced on me. I tried to grab my shell so that I could use some magic to fight back, but it was crushing me with its tentacles and I couldn't move at all. Then Princess Silva appeared," Shivana went on. "I thought she'd come to help me, but instead she and the octopus locked me in here – and then she stole my shell!"

Molly listened in horror. "She *stole* your shell?" she said. "But that's..." She broke off, feeling taken aback. "How horrible. Are you all right?"

Shivana nodded. "Yes," she said. "Just a bit shaken up. I'm so glad to see you here, Molly!"

Thoughts were spinning through Molly's mind. "You know...something strange happened with the princess last time I was a mermaid," she said slowly. "I'd just helped Pearl get her piece of the conch, when the princess appeared and asked to see it. Then she snatched it and swam off with it – but when we caught her up, she told us she was only trying to protect it for us." She frowned, trying to make sense of it all. "We managed to get it back, but I remember thinking it was weird at the time. Why would she want to steal the shells? I thought she was on our side."

Shivana looked glum. "She *is* on our side – usually," she said. "But did you notice her eyes? They were glowing red when I saw her, as bright as the octopus's eyes. The Dark Queen must have enchanted the princess, just as she has enslaved all those other creatures. And now Princess Silva is under Carlotta's control, and part of the Dark Queen's army of followers."

Molly felt sick as the truth hit her. She'd had her suspicions about the princess, but all the same... "So *she's* the one who's been spying on the Shell-Keeper mermaids," she realized. "She must have been reporting back to the Dark Queen the whole time!"

Shivana nodded. "It's shocking, isn't it? The Merqueen will be devastated. Usually the princess is the loveliest person – so sweet and generous. I hate thinking of her being under Carlotta's spell like this."

"Well, we'll have to try and rescue her," Molly said. "And we need to get your shell back from the Dark Queen. There must be a way we can break the spell on the princess and set Carlotta's army free too."

"Yes," Shivana agreed. Her eyes were full of determination now, and she tossed her mane of curls over her shoulders as if she were ready for a battle. "I hate to think of my shell in Carlotta's grasp. I don't know what she's planning to do with its powers, but I know it won't be anything good for the ocean." She put her hands on her hips. "First things first: I need to get out of here, somehow. But the icicles in this gate are rock solid – it'd be impossible for us to break or bend them. Princess Silva locked it with a key. Maybe we can use something else to pick the lock?"

Molly looked around for inspiration.

The keyhole in the gate's lock was fairly small, and she couldn't see anything that might fit it. "Maybe if we could shape a piece of ice..." she began, but even as she said the words, she knew it would be difficult. Then a thought popped into her head, as she remembered the walrus she'd seen earlier. The creature had such enormous tusks. Might it be able to use them to pull the gate open, possibly? "I've had an idea," she told Shivana. "I'll be right back."

She swam off quickly to where she'd seen the walrus before. Her heart beat a little faster as she went. What if the walrus had been enslaved by the Dark Queen, too? It might turn on her if she approached it – and those tusks were huge...

She gulped. The walrus had just eased itself back through the ice hole into the water nearby, and Molly could hear it grumbling to itself in a wheezy voice. "So tiresome! Just so tiresome!"

it was complaining. "When will it be over, oh when—"

It stopped abruptly when it saw Molly hanging back hesitantly. Then it twitched its dark whiskers and narrowed its eyes to peer at her.

"Hello, hello," it said, rather gruffly. "Where's the other one, then? Red-top. She got tired of all the ice and snow, did she, eh? On vacation in warmer waters?"

Red-top! Was he talking about Shivana? "Um..." Molly began, struck with nerves. The walrus was so big, with its long fat body, and those gigantic tusks like vampire fangs, she couldn't get her words out properly.

"Eh? Speak up! Come on, mermaid-girl, let's hear it!" barked the walrus. The way he spoke reminded Molly of her Gramps, her mom's dad, who'd been in the army back when he was younger. Thinking about Gramps, with his ramrod-straight back and his big bushy mustache, gave Molly a burst of confidence. "If you mean Shivana, that's why I came to find you," she said politely. "She's in trouble, and needs help. We were wondering..."

The walrus pushed his flippers down suddenly to send himself closer to Molly, so close that she could see the black scars and scrapes on his skin. "Trouble, eh? Our Red-top? What's happened to her, then?" he asked. Then he gave a peculiar wiggle, as if he had something on his back. "Sorry. Molting at the moment. Terribly itchy. Anyway. What was that? Speak up. Trifle deaf, these days. Tell me what I can do. At your service!"

Molly smiled thankfully. For all his gruffness, the walrus was actually rather sweet. "She's trapped – follow me," she said, swimming toward the cave, explaining what had happened as they went. The walrus swam after her, his flippers making easy work of the distance. "See?" Molly said, pointing to the barred gate at the cave entrance. "We were wondering if you could—"

But the walrus didn't need to be asked. He was already on his way to the gate, muttering fiercely to himself. "Outrageous! Outrageous! Was this Carlotta's work? How *dare* she!" Huffing with indignation he swam right up to the bars, then hooked his great tusks around two of them in a deft movement. He gave a mighty heave...and the icicles promptly cracked and broke clean away, leaving space for Shivana to swim through them, and out of her prison.

"Oh, well done!" she cried happily, throwing her arms around the walrus's large body. "Thank you so much!"

The walrus puffed up a little with pride at her words. Molly was sure he would have blushed if it were possible! "Not at all, dear girl, not at all," he said briskly. Then he did his strange squirming wiggle once more.

"If only every problem was as easy to solve," he grunted, turning and scratching his back against the rocky cave mouth. "This itching really...is... most...tiresome!"

"Ahh – are you molting?" Shivana asked knowingly. "His old winter coat is coming off," she explained to Molly. "They get terribly itchy, poor things." She picked up one of the broken icicles and began to gently scratch the walrus's back. "Poor old boy. How does that feel?"

The walrus shut his eyes.

"Marvelous," he said after a few moments. "Splendid, dear. Sheer bliss."

Shivana winked at Molly. "Well, that's the least I can do," she said. Then her face hardened. "Thanks again. We're off now to track down my shell and defeat the awful Dark Queen once and for all, so I'll see you later and—"

The walrus interrupted her with a mighty snort that sent bubbles through the water. "See you *later*? What do you mean?" he cried. "I'm coming with you, Red-top. Carlotta is no friend of mine – she's enchanted six of my friends into her army. If you're going to face her, you can't do it alone. The other walruses and I will come and help you!"

Molly was taken aback at this, but Shivana gave a grin and flung her arms around the walrus again. "You are *wonderful*," she declared fondly. "Thank you. Let's go!"

The three of them set off together through the icy water. "So…what's the plan?" Molly wondered aloud. "Do we have a plan?"

"I was just thinking about that," Shivana replied. "Carlotta could be anywhere in the ocean, but sooner or later she'll return to her cave. And that's where we're going now."

Molly's skin prickled. "Is it…is it dangerous there?"

Shivana gave a half-smile. "Afraid so," she said. "We should send word to the other Shell-Keeper mermaids and let them know what's happening. We'll need their help if we're to confront the Dark Queen."

"Leave that with me," the walrus replied immediately. "We walruses may look like fat old things, but we can swim at a fair lick when we have to, you know! I'll gather some messengers and assemble troops. Anything for the mermaids!"

"Oh, would you? That would be wonderful," Shivana said gratefully. She patted the walrus's snout. "You're a good friend. Thank you."

The walrus looked bashful and gave a barking cough. "Not at all, my dear. Happy to help. Now, if you'll excuse me...I'll go straight to Walrus Beach where all my friends will be.

I'll drag those lazy lumps into action, you just see if I don't!"

He swam off immediately, looking very purposeful as he went. Molly smiled at his departing figure as he shot through the water at great speed. To think she'd been frightened of the walrus at first, when in actual fact he'd turned out to be so kind!

Shivana was smiling, too. "He's a darling," she said, as she and Molly swam off together. "It's good to have him on our side."

The mermaids swam for a little while and soon found themselves entering a narrow icy tunnel, with rocks piled high below them and a stretch of thick ice overhead, like a white glistening ceiling. After they'd been inside the tunnel for a few moments, they heard a great pounding noise above them, as if something was trying to bash through the ice there.

"What's that?" Molly asked in alarm.

The ice was cracking and splintering over their heads. Shivana stared upward, and her mouth fell open in surprise. "I think it might be a—" she began – but before she could finish her sentence, there was an almighty crash, and the ice was smashed right through. Then, to Molly's horror, a huge creamy-white paw as big as a dinner plate plunged toward them, making a swipe for her and Shivana.

"Polar bear!" cried Shivana in alarm as a white furry face with glowing red eyes glared down at them. The Dark Queen had clearly enchanted it and turned it into a mermaid-hunter!

Shivana grabbed Molly's hand and dragged her swiftly away from the ice hole. The polar bear made another lightning-quick strike for Molly's

tail, but she swung it away just in time, her heart pounding in her ribs.

CRASH! The polar bear seemed to be following the frightened mermaids along the ice, because it was now thumping at a section in front of them. Again, the ice broke and a massive paw splashed in the cold water, its claws horribly sharp-looking.

Molly was terrified – she knew from her book that polar bears were deadly hunters. It could smell them through the ice and was using its front paws to smash through the frozen layer that separated it from the mermaids. And this polar bear was one of Carlotta's followers, enchanted to attack the mermaids at any chance!

"Come on – keep swimming," Shivana urged. She was pulling Molly frantically along and Molly realized that she'd been so frightened, she'd forgotten to swim. She gave her tail a powerful flick, pushing herself through the water as fast as she could. They had to get

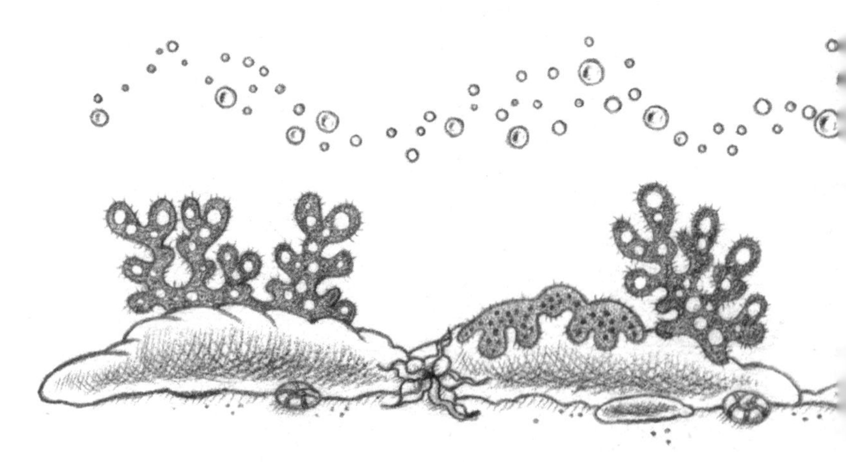

away before the polar bear had a lucky pounce.

Molly and Shivana swam on desperately, the bear thumping and smashing at the ice overhead. Luckily, the icy tunnel soon began to widen out, so they quickly veered away from the bear into deeper, open water. “He won’t be able to get us when we’re all the way down here,” Shivana reassured Molly, as they skimmed along the seabed. “Polar bears are good swimmers but they can’t hold their breath long enough to stay this deep underwater. We’re safe now.”

It took Molly a few moments to recover from the fright. Those powerful paws had been a bit too close for her liking! "I know this might sound stupid, but I feel kind of... disappointed," she confessed to Shivana. "I've always thought polar bears looked cuddly and friendly. I can't believe that one was trying to hunt us down!"

Shivana looked grave. "I know," she said. "Yes, polar bears are ferocious hunters, but they've always been like gentle giants to me. Many times I've helped the cubs learn to swim, or played tag with them. It was really scary, being on the other side, and getting chased and hunted like that." She sighed. "All the more reason we've got to defeat the Dark Queen. We have to set her army of slaves free! Come on, let's keep going. We've got a long way until we reach Carlotta's lair."

The two mermaids swam on in silence for a while. After some time, Molly noticed that the ice had all vanished and the water was becoming gradually warmer. Long emerald-green ribbons of seaweed grew up from the seabed, swaying and rippling with the current. There were more fish too – their silvery bodies forming long glittering chains in the ocean as they swam in formation. "Are we leaving the Arctic behind?" Molly asked.

Shivana nodded. "We're heading south," she replied. "We're not too far from the Dark Queen's hideout now. I've never been there before but I've heard stories about it. We all try and avoid this part of the ocean, but I know her lair is near..." She grimaced. "It's not the sort of place you want to hang around for very long. And I expect it'll be well guarded, too. We'll have to be very careful once we get closer."

Molly was about to reply, when she heard a cheerful shout from behind them. "Shivana! Molly! Wait up!"

The two mermaids turned to see a smiling blonde-haired mermaid swimming toward them.

It was Ella – the first mermaid Molly had ever met in the Undersea Kingdom – closely followed by Coral, Delphi and Pearl, the other Shell-Keepers.

Molly felt her face split into a big grin at the sight of their friendly faces. She swam over and hugged her mermaid friends in turn. "It's so good to see you!" she cried.

"And you," Pearl said, with her wide smile. Then she took Shivana's hands. "Are you all right?" she asked. "Some walruses came to find

us – they told us what had happened. I could hardly believe it!"

"Nor me," said Coral. "Did Princess Silva *really* do that to you?"

"Afraid so," Shivana said. She looked glum for a moment, then shook back her hair, as if rallying herself. "But I'm fine now, thanks to Molly and our walrus friend. Anyway, now that we're all here, let's go on together."

"Oh, it's not just the six of us," Delphi said, laughing. "Look who else has come along."

Molly and Shivana turned – and then gasped in surprise. Advancing toward them was a whole host of sea creatures. There were prancing dolphins, whales of all sizes, octopuses, squid, more types of fish than Molly could count, and of course a large group of majestic-looking walruses, their tusks shining a pale yellow through the water.

"Oh my goodness," Molly said, almost lost for words.

Shivana, too, seemed speechless for a moment. "And they're all here…for us?" she asked in amazement. "They've come to help?"

Ella nodded, her eyes bright. "Oh yes. Word's gotten around, you know. They want to defeat Carlotta just as much as we do. They've all seen friends and family captured and enslaved by her. They've come to say 'Enough's enough!'"

Molly felt quite overcome. The ocean was such an incredible place. And the fact that all of these brave creatures had joined together to oppose the Dark Queen… A lump swelled in her throat, as if she was going to cry. She bit her lip, wrestling to stay in control of her feelings. "We'd better head on, then," she said. "It looks like we have work to do."

They set off, all together. It was quite something to swim along with so many hundreds of creatures following, like an amazing marine procession. The whales were singing softly to one another, the dolphins were making excited clicks, and the walruses were bossing one another around.

Molly always found it impossible to get a sense of time while she was underwater, but it didn't feel as if they had been swimming for very long when Shivana suddenly put her finger to her lips for quiet. The creatures fell silent at once to listen.

"We're almost at the Dark Queen's cave," she said in a low voice. "See those black rocks ahead? Just the other side of them is the start of her labyrinth – a maze of rocky caves and tunnels. Carlotta lives down in the deepest, darkest chamber."

Ella spoke next. "There will be guards posted at the entrance of the labyrinth," she said, "and spies, watching out for enemies like us. From now on, we have to be quiet and cautious. Maybe it would be best if we mermaids creep into the caves to see what's happening inside. With luck, we can spy on Carlotta and form a plan. We'll send back a signal for you to join us when we need you."

The listening animals nodded their agreement. "We'll await further instructions," one of the walruses said. "Good luck!"

The six mermaids gathered by the rocks, and Delphi peeked over. "Just as we thought," she whispered, when she bobbed down again and faced the others. "Two narwhals are guarding the entrance to the labyrinth. One false move and we'll be speared, no question."

"Narwhals?" Molly repeated, confused.

Ella explained. "They're like small whales with a long sharp spike coming from their

snouts," she said. "They're fairly rare these days."

"We need a plan," Coral said. "There's no way we'll be able to slip past them. What can we do?"

Pearl twisted one of her long brown pigtails thoughtfully. "Maybe if we can distract them somehow—" she began in her gentle voice.

"I could do that," Shivana interrupted. "I'll swim around in front of them, pretending to be looking for my shell. Hopefully they'll come and chase me off and then you can sneak into the cave."

Molly felt doubtful. Shivana was being very brave, but her plan seemed rather dangerous to Molly. "Are you sure?" she asked.

Shivana nodded, her eyes glittering. "I'm sure," she said. "Don't worry, Molly, I'll lead those narwhals a merry dance all over the ocean. They won't catch me!"

"I'll come with you," Coral offered. "That way we can go in two directions, just to make things even trickier for them. And I've got my shell too, of course, in case we find ourselves in trouble."

"That sounds like a plan to me," Delphi said. "Good luck, you two!"

Molly stayed with Ella, Pearl and Delphi while Shivana and Coral swam out, closer to the Dark Queen's cave labyrinth, but still at a safe distance from the narwhals.

"Oh, where could it be?" Shivana wailed theatrically. "I've searched every corner of every ocean but still haven't found my shell!"

Molly and the other mermaids peeked over to watch. There were the two narwhals – a speckled blue-gray color, with those extraordinary spikes, similar to knights' lances. As Coral and Shivana swam back and forth a

little closer to the cave, the narwhals let out high-pitched squeals. “Stay away! You are forbidden here, enemies of Her Royal Darkness!” they cried. Then, lowering their spikes a little, they charged at the mermaids like jousting knights, surging through the water.

Molly held her breath, but Shivana and Coral were ready for the attack and peeled away in different directions. "Ooh, help!" she heard Coral scream dramatically. "Leave us alone, you big bullies!"

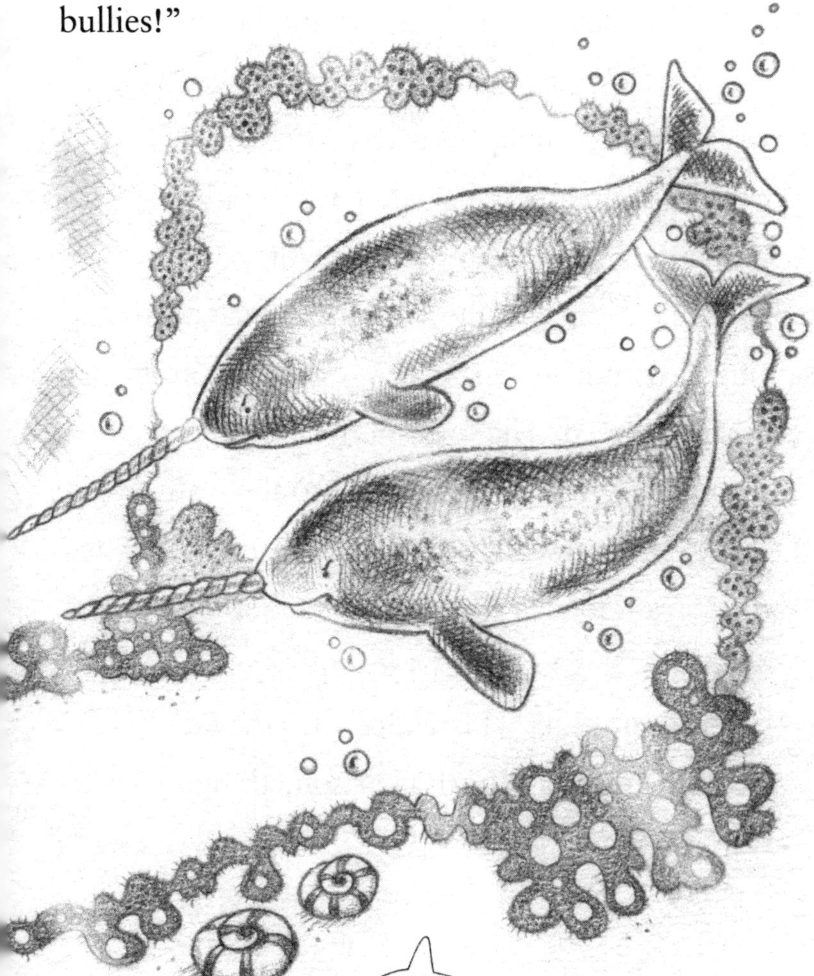

Molly felt anxious, but the other mermaids were giggling. "Fantastic," Ella said. "That'll keep those narwhals busy. Come on!"

"Are you sure Coral and Shivana will be all right?" Molly worried, as she and her friends swam quickly to the labyrinth entrance.

"They'll be fine," Pearl assured her. "They can outswim any narwhal. They're only pretending to be scared, don't worry."

The entrance to the labyrinth of caves was ringed with black rocks that dripped with mossy green seaweed. The four mermaids slipped through silently, keeping close to the walls of the tunnel inside. Molly felt her heart thump as they swam inside. It was cold and gloomy, with only faint murky light to see by.

"Listen," Ella whispered, after they'd swum further in. "I can hear something. It's Carlotta!"

They paused to listen. From far down the tunnel there came the sound of a distant voice, muffled and echoing. Then came a tremendous roar of many voices together.

Molly gulped. "It sounds like her whole army is with her," she hissed nervously.

"Let's creep closer so we can hear what she's saying," Delphi suggested.

They swam silently along the dark tunnels, which forked several times. It wasn't long before Molly had completely lost her bearings as they took one turn after another. At one point, Molly felt something slimy brush her bare arms and almost cried out in fear until she realized it was only seaweed drifting against her, like thin green fingers.

Carlotta's voice was louder now and more distinct, and suddenly Ella, who was leading the way, stopped dead and motioned for the others

to do the same. "Just around this corner," she said in a tiny voice, pointing to where the tunnel curved away to the right.

She cautiously put her head around the rocky wall. Molly, Delphi and Pearl did the same. Molly's heart stepped up a beat as she saw what was on the other side. A huge cavern, with the Dark Queen herself at one end, a black swirling cloak around her, and a glowing piece of shell held triumphantly in her hand. She had long black hair, a hooked nose and several warts on her face. Her eyes were cold and black.

In front of her, staring up with adoring red eyes, were masses of followers. Whales, sharks, jellyfish, snakes, eels…the cavern was almost bursting with them all. And there, right in the front row, Molly could just make out Princess Silva, gazing up at the wicked Dark Queen as if she was under a spell. *Which of course she is,* Molly reminded herself with a shudder.

Then Molly heard what the Dark Queen was saying, and an icy chill went down her spine.

"That secret mermaid almost ruined everything," Carlotta cried, a fist clenched in rage. "A mere child, too! She and those Shell-Keepers thought they could get the better of me, but I have triumphed at the last. For here is the piece of shell I wanted most of all!" She held up Shivana's piece of the conch, her voice rich with gloating. "With the magic of this, I can make sure the ice at the ends of the earth melts completely. Land will be flooded everywhere – and then there will be even more sea for me to rule over!"

The four mermaids drew back in horror. No one wanted to see or hear any more. This was awful news. "We've got to stop her," Delphi said, her voice shaking. "Let's get out of here before we're discovered and make a plan.

We must get Shivana's shell back before the Dark Queen causes any damage."

"Did you see how many followers she has?" Pearl asked glumly as they swam back toward the entrance of the labyrinth. "She has so much protection – it will be almost impossible to grab the shell from her."

"Can we do something with *our* shells?" Molly suggested. "I mean, we've got five pieces, and the Dark Queen only has one, so..."

They were approaching the cave entrance now and they all fell silent, pressing themselves against the wall as they went, just in case the narwhals were back on patrol. There was no creature in sight though, so the mermaids slipped back through the rocky opening and darted for cover behind the same stretch of rocks as before.

"Look, there are Coral and Shivana," Ella said, pointing into the distance, where the narwhals were still grimly chasing the mermaids, who kept swerving in all directions.

"So, what are we going to do?" Delphi asked after a moment. "I think Molly's right – we should use the magic of our shells. Now that our five pieces are back together, we could try making an arch of power – what do you think?"

"An arch of power, yes!" cried Pearl. Her eyes were shining and her words tumbled out excitedly. "With all the animals who've come to help passing underneath it, to make the magic even stronger." She put two fingers in her mouth and gave a piercing whistle, then bobbed behind the rocks, pulling the others down with her. "Just wanted Coral and Shivana to know that we're out of the cave," she explained.

Molly was feeling a little lost in the conversation. "What's an arch of power?" she asked uncertainly. "And how will that help?"

"It's the strongest form of mermaid magic conjured up by the conch," Ella explained.

"It would normally be done with all six pieces, but we can try it with the five we have. We put them together and make an arch shape, with three of us on each side. Then as the creatures swim through our arch, they add strength to the magic. Together we can call upon the ocean for help."

"But what will happen to Carlotta?" Molly asked, still feeling confused. "I don't see how..."

"A whirlpool, that should do it!" Delphi exclaimed. "We'll try to summon a whirlpool which will hopefully drag her out of the cave. If she's caught up in that, she won't be able to do any more magic!"

"What about the animals?" Molly asked, remembering the army of creatures she'd seen inside Carlotta's chamber. "Will they be all right?"

Pearl nodded. "We will concentrate our

power and make sure the whirlpool is just for Carlotta," she said. "Then we can break the enchantment, so the other creatures and Princess Silva will be fine."

Coral and Shivana swam up just then, grinning. "That was fun," Shivana said. "What's happening? Any news?"

"Yes," chorused the others.

"We've got a plan," Ella added, beaming.

A few minutes later, the six mermaids were in position, in open water, out of sight of the narwahls. Delphi, Coral and Pearl were on one side, holding their shells in front of them, arms outstretched in the water. Molly, Ella and Shivana were opposite them, doing the same thing, although Shivana's hands were empty, of course.

"One, two, three...now!" cried Coral, and they all moved a fraction closer so that the five

pieces of conch touched in the center of their mermaid arch. As the shells came together, there was an incredible crackling sound, and sparks of rainbow-colored light went shooting through the water. *It's just like fireworks*, Molly thought, her eyes wide.

Her shell was warm in her hand and she could feel the heat from her friends' shells radiating out too, as if they were generating enormous magical powers.

The mermaids slowly moved their shells apart, and a rainbow arch formed between them. The sea creatures who'd come to support the mermaids began to pass under the arch, one by one, and the shells glowed brighter still, fizzling with extra magic each time.

It felt to Molly almost as if her conch was alive, vibrating in her hands like a huge buzzing insect that wanted to be let free. Her arms ached with the effort of holding it up, but she hung on, knowing that the mermaid power was growing stronger all the time.

Finally, when the last turtle had swum through the arch, Shivana spoke. "This should do the trick," she said, and recited a chant. When all the Shell-Keepers had learned it, they chorused as one:

"*By the power of the conch,*
We call upon the waves
To seize Queen Carlotta
And to set free her slaves!"

The shells crackled with energy and the seawater around them was flooded with dazzling lights and colors for a moment. Then they saw it – the whirlpool, gathering strength

beneath the arch and moving toward the edge of the caves.

The six mermaids swam together, pushing the whirlpool forward, their shells still glowing brightly with magic.

Into the cave they went, and through the maze of tunnels that led to the large chamber where they'd seen the Dark Queen and her army. Molly felt sick with nerves. How she hoped their magic was strong enough! If the whirlpool failed to seize the Dark Queen, then she was sure to turn on them – as would her followers.

On they went through the tunnels, the whirlpool spinning ahead of them, sparkling with magic. Then, with one final push, they rounded the corner...and sent the whirlpool straight at Carlotta!

She screamed in horror as she saw it and tried to dodge away, but before she could move, it had enveloped her.

Molly watched as Carlotta was dragged into the whirlpool, which spun her around so fast her cape whipped around her like a giant black bandage, preventing her from moving her arms or tail.

"Now I can get my shell back," Shivana said, swimming across to the whirlpool. It was difficult for Shivana to push herself forward, but gradually she got closer to Carlotta. Then she held up her hand in front of her, and Molly saw all the other mermaids raise their shells. She copied them and, with a flash of light, Shivana's piece of the magical conch burst from the whirlpool and soared through the water into Shivana's waiting hand.

"Yes!" cried Shivana joyfully. "Now to finish her off...let's join all six shell pieces together!"

Shivana joined the other Shell-Keepers at a safe distance from the whirling Dark Queen, and held her conch piece upward. Ella, Delphi, Coral and Pearl all did the same, so that the five conch pieces fit together. Molly copied them, making the conch complete for the first time since she'd become a secret mermaid.

The conch shone brightly and Molly felt happiness burst through her at the sight. They'd done it. They'd actually done it!

Now that the conch was whole again, its magic seemed to be affecting Carlotta even more.

"Help!" she shrieked, as what looked like black wisps of smoke began leaking out from her spinning figure.

"What's happening?" Molly asked, watching in alarm.

"Her bad spells are being dissolved," Delphi replied with a smile. "All her enchantments are breaking!"

The Dark Queen gave a scream of rage and shook her hands free of the cape, clawing toward the Shell-Keepers in fury. "I'll get you for this!" she screeched. "You haven't seen the last of me. I'll—" But before she could finish, the whirlpool picked her up and spun her right through the chamber and out of the labyrinth, toward the open ocean.

The Shell-Keepers broke apart, and Shivana and Pearl followed Carlotta. Molly stayed where she was though. She'd just noticed that as the Dark Queen's enchantments had broken, the eyes of her army had returned to their normal colors. The killer whale which had attacked Ella so violently was there, blinking and staring around as if it had just woken from a long sleep.

The shark which had chased Molly and Delphi let out a toothy yawn and slid out of the cavern meekly. And there was Princess Silva, looking confused and afraid...until she spotted the mermaids, that was.

"What am I doing here?" she cried, swimming over to them. "I feel as if I've had the strangest dream."

"You're safe now," Coral told her, hugging the princess. "We've come to take you home. All of you!" she added, raising her voice to address the other creatures. "Your friends and family are waiting outside. Come, follow us. We will take you there."

Molly and her mermaid friends led the way through the rocky tunnels of the labyrinth, followed by the many creatures who'd once been part of the Dark Queen's army.

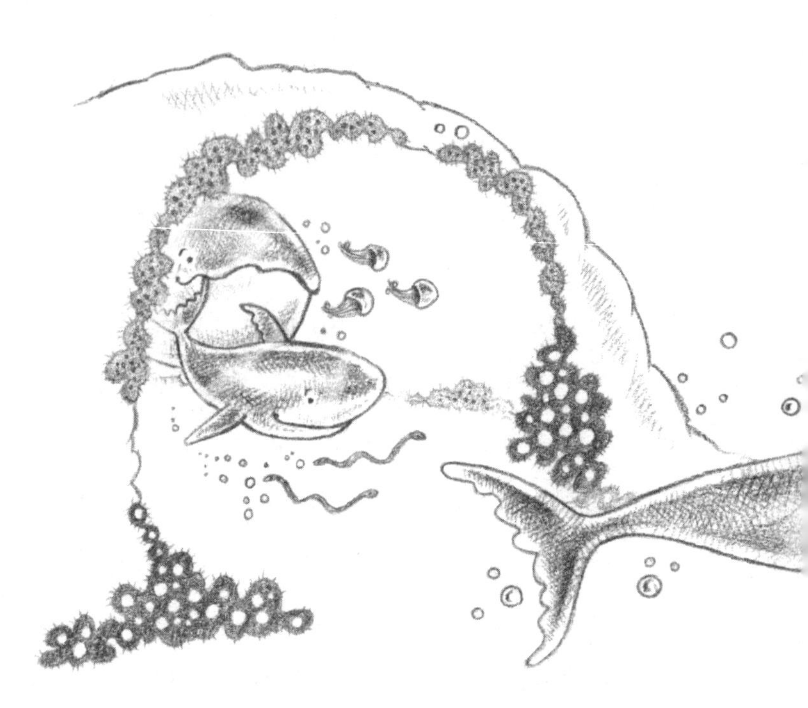

Out they all went into the light once more, where there was great excitement and happy exclamations from the waiting animals. Octopuses hugged one another, getting into tangled knots and laughing happily. Whales snuggled up to each other, making joyful singing noises. And the walruses slapped their tusks together, and scratched each other's itchy backs.

Molly gazed around, unable to stop smiling.

Then, in the distance, she caught sight of the Dark Queen being whirled away, still trapped in the whirlpool. One by one, all the other Shell-Keepers turned to watch too. "What's going to happen to her now?" Molly asked.

"The whirlpool will take her far from here," Shivana said. "When the enchantments were broken it weakened her, so I should think she'll lay low for a long time." She smiled at Molly and hugged her impulsively. "I am so glad you rescued me from that cave, Molly. None of this would have been possible without you!"

"It's true," came a familiar voice. Molly spun around to see the Merqueen herself swimming gracefully toward them. "My dear, I have just come from the palace, where I watched events unfold on my Seeing Stone. You have done wonderfully, Molly, and we are

preparing a feast in your honor. All our animal friends are invited to celebrate the banishing of the Dark Queen!"

A deafening cheer went up at her words, and Queen Luna smiled. "And now, where is my daughter?"

"I'm here! Oh, Mother!" Princess Silva looked as if she was close to tears as she swam toward the Merqueen, her arms outstretched. Mother and daughter came together and held each other tight.

"You're safe now, I've got you," Molly heard the Merqueen murmur into her daughter's hair. "Oh, Silva, I've been so worried!"

Shivana swam up to Molly and slipped an arm through hers. "Not bad going, secret mermaid," she said, her eyes twinkling. "You rescued me, escaped from a polar bear, and helped banish the Dark Queen and free her slaves. And now there's a mermaid party and banquet to look forward to. That's what I call a busy day!"

"Absolutely," Ella said, joining the conversation. "You did so well, Molly. We're proud to have you as one of the Shell-Keepers."

"Couldn't have put it better myself," Coral chimed in, giving Molly a friendly nudge.

Molly felt as if she might very well burst with pride. "Thank you," she said. "I'm so happy I'm a secret mermaid – I love my adventures with all of you."

Delphi winked. "Glad to hear it," she said. "Because I'm sure you'll have many, many more!"

"But no more adventures today," Pearl laughed. "Just partying! Come on, let's go to the palace. We can teach you all our favorite party games."

There came a small cough from behind them, and Molly turned to see the friendly walrus there, looking puffed up and solemn about something. "Before you all go, I'd like to say a few words," he announced.

"Oh, here we go," a naughty seal pup muttered to its friend. "We'll be here for hours now!"

"My dear," the walrus said to Molly, pretending not to hear the seal, "not only have you helped defeat Carlotta, but you have also helped to set free many, many sea creatures today."

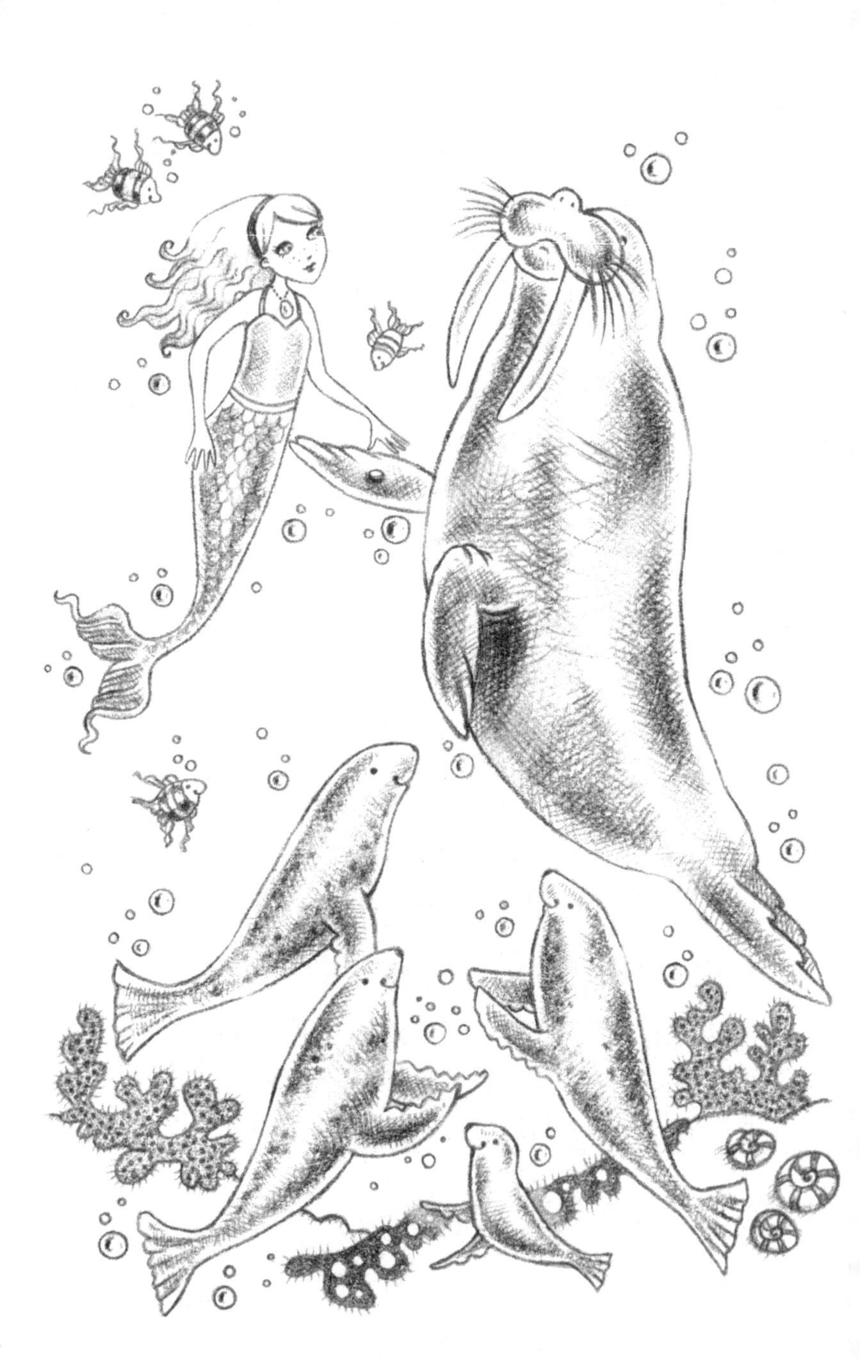

A cheer went up at the words and several sea lions clapped their flippers together in splashy applause.

"Because of this, we would like to declare you a special friend of sea creatures everywhere, and present you with a small gift," the walrus went on, and held out a flipper. "Here," he said. "Take it. It's to go on your necklace."

Molly swam over to see that he was holding out a small silvery disc on his flipper. "Th-thank you," she said, almost lost for words at the surprise gift. The disc shone all colors as she picked it up and fastened it to her necklace. "Thank you so much."

The walrus bowed his head solemnly. "A great pleasure," he assured her. "And from now on, if you are ever in trouble in the ocean, one of us will always come to your rescue."

Molly smiled at him, feeling a rush of great joy. It was wonderful to be thanked by all the creatures of the ocean for her part in the adventure. Even more wonderful was that she and the other Shell-Keepers had defeated the Dark Queen together, and that all the pieces of the magical conch were back with their rightful owners.

Best of all, it was so exciting to think that even more adventures lay ahead! She grinned to herself and somersaulted in the water. She really was the luckiest girl in the world!

The Secret Mermaid

To find out more
about Molly and all her
mermaid friends, and have
some magical ocean fun,
check out

www.secret-mermaid.com

Sue Mongredien has published over 60 books, including the magical *Oliver Moon, Junior Wizard* series. Like Molly Holmes, Sue loves exploring, and gave up a job as an editor of children's books to travel the world, before becoming a full-time writer. Sue also loves the sea, and had a house near Brighton beach in England before moving to Bath, also in England, where she now lives with her husband and three children.